That's a Good Idea

Amina Blackwood Meeks, Ph.D

Illustrations by
Jagath Kosmodara

Brer Anancy Press

First Printing, 2021
ISBN: 978-9768266118

Ordering Information:
Quantity sales. Special discounts are available on quantity purchases by corporations, associations, and others. For details, contact:

Brer Anancy Press
Ocho Rios, St. Ann,
Jamaica, W.I
info@breranancypress.com
www.BrerAnancyPress.com

Printed in the United States of America

THIS BOOK BELONGS TO

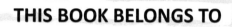

Our storytelling tradition comes to us from West Africa.
We inherited the special way for opening our stories.
The storyteller makes the call, and the audience responds.

Crick! – Crack!
Tim, Tim! - Bois Seche!
E di Kwik! - E di Kwak!
Nanse! - Tory!

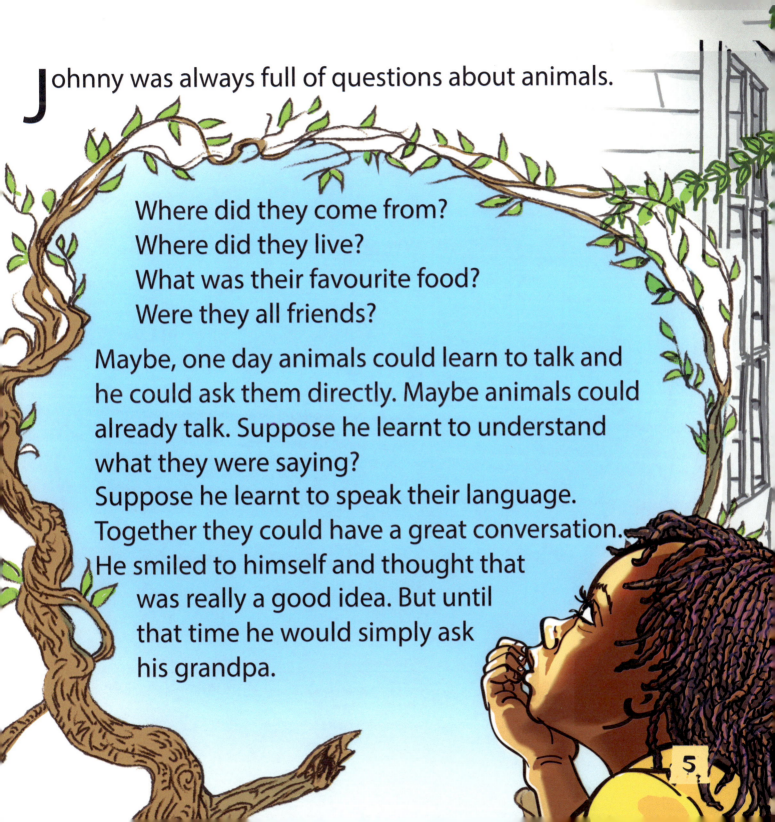

Johnny was always full of questions about animals.

Where did they come from?
Where did they live?
What was their favourite food?
Were they all friends?

Maybe, one day animals could learn to talk and he could ask them directly. Maybe animals could already talk. Suppose he learnt to understand what they were saying?
Suppose he learnt to speak their language. Together they could have a great conversation. He smiled to himself and thought that was really a good idea. But until that time he would simply ask his grandpa.

6

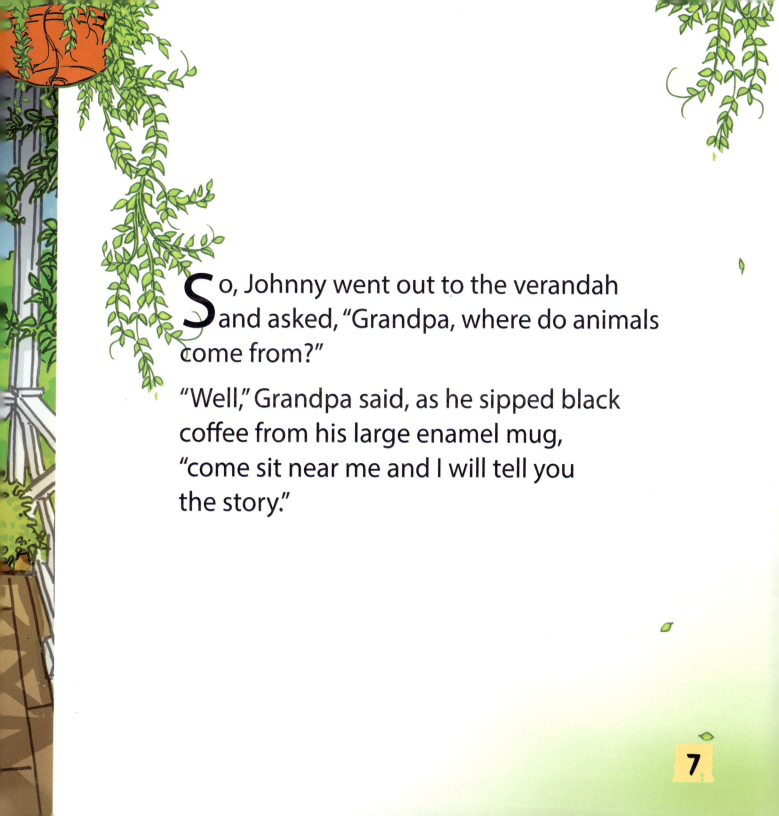

So, Johnny went out to the verandah and asked, "Grandpa, where do animals come from?"

"Well," Grandpa said, as he sipped black coffee from his large enamel mug, "come sit near me and I will tell you the story."

It all started with Great Spirit. Before a long, long time ago Great Spirit decided to make mountains.

High mountains
Low mountains
Brown mountains
Red mountains
Black mountains
Green mountains.

But there was only one Blue Mountain.
Down the side of Blue Mountain,
Great Spirit decided to put some rivers.

Slow River
Swift River
Black River
White River
Mango River
Cane River.

Cane River was Great Spirit's favourite, because
of the plan that one day, it would be a wonderful
place for Bob to wash his dreads and cook.

However, before Bob came to enjoy Cane River, Great Spirit would sit on its banks everyday thinking up other things to create.

Maaga dawg,
Stray cat
Ratbat
And sisserou chatty mout parrot.
Goat
Sensei fowl
Crapeau
And screech owl.
Cow
Alligator
Green monkey
And mongoose.

The mention of Mongoose made Johnny laugh. "I know Mongoose," he said, "that's the animal that chases rats out of the cane-fields. It's always running across the road, without even looking. And most of the time, it's alone. Except when it is carrying Bedward's chicken in its mouth." And to prove how much he knew Johnny broke out into song.

Mongoose go inna Bedward kitchen
Teck out one a him righteous chicken
Put it inna him waistcoat pockit
Sly mongoose...🎵🎶🎵

Grandpa nodded, joined in the chorus and then continued his story.

"Well without a chicken, Mongoose looked so lonely because he was always alone. That is why Great Spirit decided to allow Mongoose to make one last animal, so he could have a friend, just to keep him company. And Mongoose said..."

Johnny jumped right in, "Mmmm, that's a good idea."

According to Grandpa, Great Spirit said to Mongoose, "Tell you what, take this piece of modelling clay and make me a model of what you think the last animal on earth should look like. It's time I had a rest."

"And what do you think Mongoose said?" asked Grandpa. Johnny was ready with the answer, "Mmmm, that's a good idea!" Grandpa continued,

"And off Mongoose went with his lump of modelling clay until he met Worm."

Worm called out, "Hey, Mongoose, where did you get all that clay?"

"From Great Spirit!" Mongoose shouted so the entire forest could hear. He was so proud to make it known that he was a personal friend of Great Spirit.

Mongoose continued to boast. "Would you believe the Maximum Creator ran out of ideas of things to make? Sure did. He asked me to make a model of what the last animal on earth should look like."

"Oh, that's easy," responded Worm, "no other animal can wriggle like me." And he strutted his stuff to prove it.

One wriggle of a bele, two wriggles of a que-que and for brawta, four wriggles of a dinki-mini. "So there," he said, feeling all satisfied, "the last animal on earth should look like me, of course."

And Mongoose said, "Mmmm, that's a good idea."

Grandpa explained that Mongoose gave Worm a piece of the modelling clay and promised to return later in the day to see what he made. Then off he went. Soon he met Lion.

"Mongoose," Lion roared as loudly as he could, trying to show his super-power as a proud, perfectly-made beast, "from whence came forth such a huge lump of modelling clay?" Johnny smiled at Grandpa's imitation of Lion's regal speech in this old-fashioned way of speaking. But he didn't interrupt. So Grandpa continued.

"Of course Mongoose was only too happy to talk about his friendship with Great Spirit. This time he stated that he was Great Spirit's Assistant Creative Director. As Mongoose told his story, Lion began preening. He flicked his head and shook his glorious mane. He declared that having the most gorgeous hairstyle of all the animals in the forest, - except maybe for Bob – was very important.

Therefore, the last animal must look like him, of course. And Mongoose said?" Johnny piped up, "Mmmm that's a good idea."

"Right you are," answered Grandpa, "so Lion got his piece of the clay."

Johnny listened as Grandpa related that not long after that Mongoose met Donkey. As soon as their eyes met, Mongoose burst into a song which Grandpa was delighted to sing to Johnny.

Tell me which mont de dankey kean call

Which a de mont de donkey kean call

Tell me which mont de dankey kean call

Which a de mont de donkey kean call.

January, February, March, April

May, June, July, Haw-he-haw-he-haw....♫♪♪

Now Donkey had a bad lisp. But according to Grandpa, donkey didn't care to be reminded of his speech impediment. He would rather show off his perfect teeth. In addition, he thought he had the best singing voice anyone could imagine. And seeing that some people called him "Dankey" while others called him "Jackass," he had secretly renamed himself D-J. So, he quickly interrupted with a question about the purpose of the lump of modelling clay. When he got the answer, he naturally suggested that the last animal on earth should look like him.

An de Jackass a walk an bray

Meck him bray, meck him bray.

Haw-haw-haw...♪♫♪♪

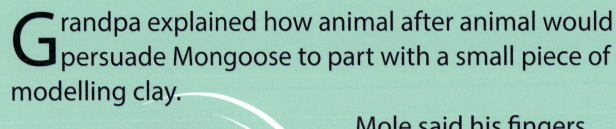

Grandpa explained how animal after animal would persuade Mongoose to part with a small piece of modelling clay.

Mole said his fingers were the most delicate and sensitive, designed to give everyone the gentlest touch.

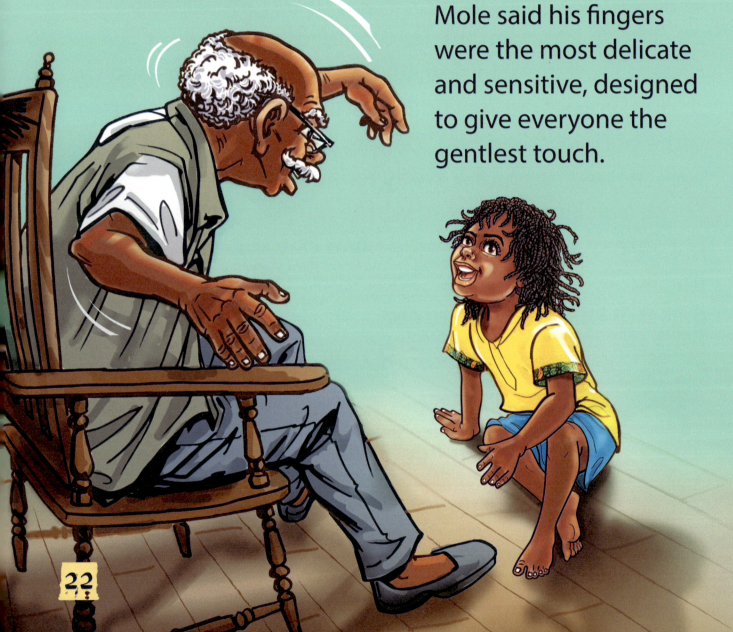

Eagle said she had the most beautiful eyes for the look of kindness.

Every time an animal gave a reason why the last animal on earth should be their look-a-like, Mongoose said: "Mmmm, that's a good idea," beamed Johnny.

23

This continued until the clay was all done. In the meantime, Great Spirit had grown impatient waiting for Mongoose to return. Then one day Mongoose heard someone yelling his name.

"Mongoose!" It was Great Spirit.

Mongoose came running, "Yes, Great Spirit, yes."

"Where is the model of the last animal on earth?" demanded Great Spirit.

"Well," Mongoose began slowly, "Worm had a really good reason why it should look like him so I gave him a piece of clay. And then Lion had such a fabulous hairstyle, and D-J had a song and a dance and Mole touched me ever so gently, just what the world needs, gentle touches...and then...well... everyone had a good reason, so I'm out of clay and they are all out there modelling."

Then Mongoose had a brilliant idea. The words tumbled out of his mouth faster than his mind could figure out what he was really saying.

"With all these models, Great Spirit, one day you and I can launch a special line of garments and have the greatest fashion show in the world. We could discover the next supermodel. Oh, I can see it now. Paparazzi! Lights! Camera! Action! Tourists would come from everywhere. Oh, Great Spirit, how about a beauty contest? We could dress up all the animals in the most amusing outfits and ask them some test questions. Now, how would we decide who would be the winner? We could play Mirror, Mirror on the wall..."

Great Spirit roared and cut him off right there, "Mongoose, that's the stupidest thing I've ever heard." But Mongoose protested, "Mmmmm, but it's a good idea."

That made Great Spirit mad. And when Great Spirit got mad:

Lightnin an tunder,

Brimstone an fire,

Judgement awaiting what a woe....♫♪♪♩

And as Grandpa sang Great Spirit's response, Johnny clapped his hands and danced. He loved Grandpa's singing.

"And rains." Grandpa continued, "Whenever Great Spirit was upset it brought down the rains."
Grandpa started singing again.

What a hebby rain an breeze, oh

What a heap a dutty water

What a hebby rain a fall...♫♪♪♩

The rains wet up all the models that the animals had put out to dry and they began to fall apart.

Mongoose ran around trying to put them back together, singing a song of his own.

Dally man dally man dally man wan

Dally man dally man dally man two

Yu nuh hear Tukuma say draw back one. ♫♪♪

He picked up a little piece of model from this one and another piece from that one and piece more and before he knew what he was doing he had rubbed all the pieces together into one. Then he found a cave and he put the model in there to dry.

And Tim! Tim! Bois Seche! One day when it was dry, dry, dry, he took it out and carried it to Great Spirit.

"Seet here, Great Spirit. Seet dey now, yu seet deh now, yu seet deh now, yu seet. This is the model of the last animal on earth."

Great Spirit looked at the beautiful eyes of that model, the rich, deep complexion and the perfect teeth. Great Spirit loved the hairstyle. Oh it could wriggle and it could sing. Great Spirit had his own song.

Nuh tease him, no worry him

Nuh meck de hamper squeeze him...♫♪♪

Then Great Spirit looked at that animal some more. All the while poor Mongoose was rubbing his paws anxiously waiting for Great Spirit to make a decision. When he could no longer hold back his excitement he blurted out:

"So how is it, Great Spirit? What you think?"

Grandpa turned to Johnny,
"So what do you think Great Spirit said?"

Before Johnny could reply, Grandpa surprised him with a new response.
"Lawd! Black people pretty, sah. Up! You mighty race. Meck me clap meself."

And Mongoose said, "Mmmm, that's a good idea."

Johnny thought the best idea of all was the great
big hug they shared at the end of the story,
just before Grandpa sneaked him
a wee little sip of coffee from the
great big enamel mug.

Made in the USA
Columbia, SC
09 February 2025

52838761R00022